THE MANY ADVENTURES OF

LIAM

AND

MARCOS

THE MONKEY

MELISSA FERREIRA-RODRIGUEZ

PAGE PUBLISHING, INC.
Conneaut Lake, PA

First originally published by Page Publishing 2020

ISBN 978-1-64628-404-7 (pbk)
ISBN 978-1-64628-405-4 (digital)

Printed in the United States of America

To my husband William and son Liam,
who inspire me everyday, thank you.

A long, long time ago, in a land far, far away, there lived a little prince named Liam. Liam lived in a giant sparkly castle with Mommy Queen and Daddy King. Liam also had a pet monkey who had red and white stripes, big ears, and a long tail. His name was Marcos. Marcos was Liam's best friend. Marcos wore shiny silver knight armor and was by Liam's side day and night to protect him.

Liam and Marcos enjoyed spending their days playing hide-and-seek and tag throughout the castle. They enjoyed playing with the many toys Liam owned. Liam especially enjoyed reading bedtime stories with Marcos, Mommy Queen and Daddy King. Marcos was like the brother Liam didn't have.

One day, Marcos noticed Liam seemed a bit sad.

"What's wrong?" asked Marcos.

"I don't want to play with these toys anymore. I want new toys," said Liam.

"Can you please take me to Toy Land?" asked Liam.

"Only if Mommy Queen and Daddy King agree," replied Marcos.

Liam ran through the castle to search for Mommy Queen and Daddy King. He was so excited because he just knew they would say yes!

"You have more than enough toys, my sweet little boy," said Mommy Queen. Liam didn't like this response.

"But I always get new toys!" cried Liam.

"How about you use some of your own gold coins from your allowance to buy a new toy, my boy?" Daddy King suggested.

Liam's frown turned upside down, and he smiled with joy. "I have plenty of gold coins saved up," said Liam. "Come on, Marcos, let's go to Toy Land!"

Liam ran through the castle to his room, to his green piggy bank, and shook his gold coins out. He had enough saved up to buy a couple of toys! Liam grabbed a red velvety bag and threw the coins inside. "Let's go, Marcos!"

"Are you sure you want to spend it all?" asked Marcos.

"Yes!" said Liam. "Let's go to Toy Land!"

They got inside the carriage that was pulled by green-and-white-striped horses, and they rode over the cotton candy high hills, through Candy Forest filled with candy cane trees, lollipop flowers, and gumdrop bushes, past the chocolate river, and up the ice cream mountain— they finally made it to Toy Land!

Toy Land was every little prince's dream! It had every toy you could dream of!

Liam and Marcos ran up and down the aisles, pulling toys off the shelves. Marcos was carrying so many toys he almost fell over! Liam passed his gold coins to the workers to pay for his toys.

"Are you sure you want to spend all your gold coins?" asked Marcos.

"Yes!" said Liam with such excitement. "Let's pay for the toys and head back to the castle to play."

So they paid the gold coins and packed the horse and carriage with the toys and off they went over the ice cream mountain, through the chocolate river, through Candy Forest, but as they passed the candy cane trees and the lollipop flowers and the gumdrop bushes, Liam noticed his green-and-white-striped horses slow down.

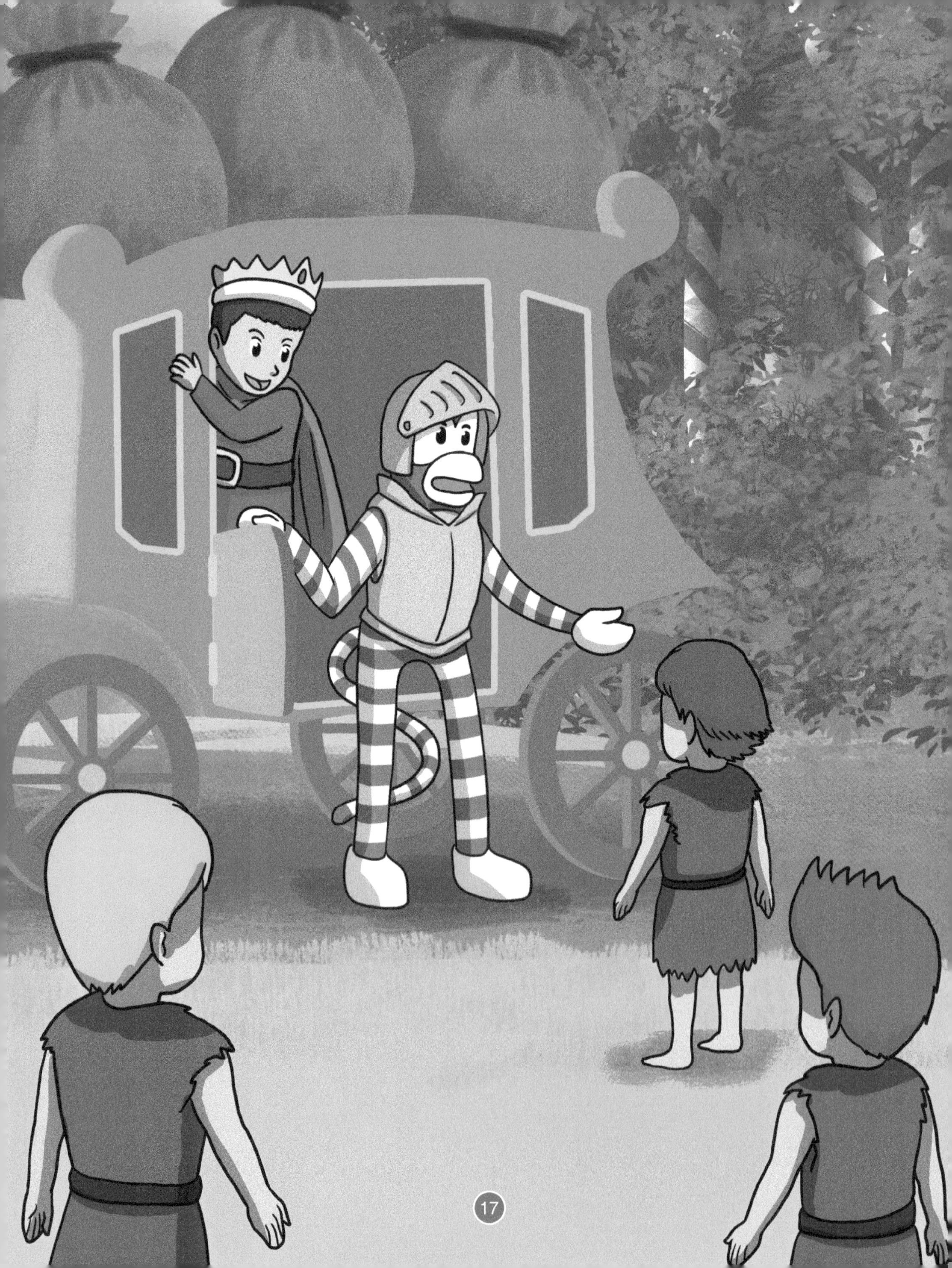

"Why have we stopped?" Liam asked Marcos.

"Stay here. I'll check," said Marcos.

Marcos got off the carriage to find the horse and carriage surrounded by children from the Candy Forest Village.

Liam popped his head out and saw the children standing there. "Hello, friends!" said Liam.

"Would you like to play?" Liam was excited to see so many children! They started off by playing hide-and-seek and tag, and then they ate some candy canes off the candy cane tree for dessert. Liam then wanted to play with his new toys and his new friends.

"Go get your toys, and I'll go get my new toys out of my carriage so we can play!"

Liam ran back to the carriage but noticed the children weren't moving.

"What's wrong?" asked Liam. "Don't you want to play with me?"

"We do," said one of the little boys, "but we don't own any toys."

"Yeah, we've never even been to Toy Land," said a little girl. "We only play tag or hide-and-seek in Candy Forest for fun."

This made Liam sad. He wanted to open his new, shiny toys and take them out of the box to play with his new friends.

But then Liam realized something. It made him even sadder that his friends didn't have their own toys to love and play with.

"What's wrong?" asked Marcos.

"Marcos, I want to give my new friends a gift. I want to give them my new toys. I have enough toys at home, like Mommy Queen and Daddy King said. I want my friends to be happy like me."

"That sounds like a lovely idea," said Marcos.

And so Liam gifted his new friends all the new, shiny toys he had just bought from Toy Land.

The children were excited and thanked Liam. They made Liam promise to come back and play with them, and they would share the toys with him.

So back in the carriage they went, and Marcos and Liam continued their journey through Candy Forest and over the cotton candy high hills until they reached the giant sparkly castle. Once inside, Liam told Mommy Queen and Daddy King of the adventure he had that day. He even asked how he could earn more gold coins so he could go back to Toy Land and buy more toys, but this time, not for himself, but for the children of the village, who didn't have any. He even offered to pass along some of his toys that he no longer played with.

Mommy Queen, Daddy King, and Marcos the Monkey grinned from ear to ear as they heard Liam speak of the adventure he had with Marcos the Monkey, because they knew he had learned a valuable lesson that day, and this filled their hearts with joy.

The End

ABOUT THE AUTHOR

Melissa Ferreira-Rodriguez is from the Bronx, New York where she currently resides with her husband, William, and their son, Liam. Melissa loves spending time with her family and creating memories for her son. Her husband has always had a love for monkeys, which quickly grew on Melissa when they started dating, and then on their son when he was born. Both her husband and son helped inspire her creation for the characters Liam and Marcos the Monkey.

This is Melissa's first children's book, and she hopes the first of many to come. She wants to be able to create something memorable for her son to always cherish. She hopes children will learn lessons from her books that they can use with them in real life. She wants to be able to make children and adults smile and laugh when reading her books, just like her husband and son make her smile and laugh every day, as she believes laughter is the best form of therapy.

CPSIA information can be obtained
at www.ICGtesting.com
Printed in the USA
BVHW062000100321
602124BV00014B/764